Hello Pine Lake!

Sarah E. Huiskes

Illustrations by Sarah Sivright

Tasora

ISBN 978-1-948192-16-3
Printed in the United States of America

Book Design and Typesetting by Wendy Holdman
Printed at Bookmobile, Minneapolis, MN

Tasora Books
5120 Cedar Lake Road S.
Minneapolis, MN 55416
(952) 345-4488
Distributed by Itasca Books

This book is dedicated to my dear Grandpa Ed
who was always generous with his time and his love.
He shared his appreciation and respect for nature
with wisdom and humility. His spirit is with me always.

I see the bright morning sun peek through the windows and smile when I awake because I remember today is the day we are going to Pine Lake.

The drive seems so long because of my growing excitement with each familiar turn on the road. My grandpa keeps the radio on to listen to the baseball game. I begin to start planning my adventures at Pine Lake. This is a place that is familiar, yet seems brand new each time I visit.

As we pull onto the road that takes us closer to Pine Lake, my grandfather slows down the car and it seems like we're barely moving. "We have to keep an eye out for deer," my grandpa says. When we see a deer in the meadow, we stop the car, keep quiet, and watch what my grandpa calls a "beautiful creature." This deer is the first to welcome us to Pine Lake.

As we approach the driveway, we roll down our windows to feel the clean and cool air. We slowly make our way down the long driveway until I begin to see the beautiful blue water and yell, "Hello, Pine Lake!" I jump out of the car and feel a sense of freedom in the air. As I look around, I see woods to explore and adventures to create.

We head down to the dock to look out at the water and breathe in the beauty of Pine Lake. All of a sudden, we hear a SPLASH and see circles ripple through the water. I wonder what made that splash? I look in the water and see a school of sunfish around the dock. I think the fish knew I had arrived at Pine Lake and remembered I usually bring bread with me to the dock to feed them. The fish will have to wait. It is time to get into the water!

My grandpa is the first one in the water. As he dives in, he barely makes a splash. When it is my turn, he exclaims, "4, 3, 2, 1, GO!" I start running down the dock and leap as high as I can into the air. I feel the cool water hit my feet and surround me as I go under water. I swim to the surface and smile because the water of Pine Lake makes me feel free.

My grandpa swims beside me and we head toward the raft. As we feel the warm sun shining down, I ask my grandpa, "Do you think I will ever be able to swim across the lake by myself?" My grandpa smiles and says, "I certainly do." He says, "Pine Lake is a beautiful place that teaches you something new every day." I ask him, "What did Pine Lake teach you today, Grandpa?" And he says, "We will see."

As we sit down for lunch, I look over to the railing and see a fuzzy creature moving. "Grandpa, it's Charlina! I was hoping she would stop by. Grandpa, Charlina visits me every time I come to Pine Lake." Grandpa says, "It sounds like Pine Lake is Charlina's home and you are her friend."

I make a small home for Charlina in a jar with lots of leaves and twigs and my grandpa reminds me that when it is time to leave Pine Lake, we need to place Charlina back in the woods, which is her real home. I always wish I could take her home with me, but I know that her real home is in the woods at Pine Lake.

As we get ready for our canoe ride, we make sure to pack the binoculars. Grandpa holds the canoe steady so I can get in and hands me my paddle. As my grandpa sits in the canoe he says, "Remember as we paddle around the lake, the creatures will only say hello if we are quiet visitors."

"OK, Grandpa," I say.

As we start paddling through the water, I look down and see bright green seaweed and reach my hand in to feel the plants in the water. My hand brushes against the slimy side of a lily pad and I start to giggle. But then I remember we need to be quiet and I look at my grandpa and he smiles.

My grandpa says, "Look! There is a turtle on that log."
I try hard to see the turtle but could not find it on the log,
so I take my binoculars and look across the water toward
the log and see it. I see a small green turtle with its neck
stretched high as if he is saying hello to us. And then,
in that moment he crawled back into the water.

As we round the corner of the lake, my grandpa says this part of the lake is called Heron's Cove. He says, "Keep watch for a beautiful blue heron who may be here with us." I ask him, "How will I know when I see one?" My grandpa says, "Look for a tall blue bird with a large wing-span." I grab my binoculars and search the cove. As I search the weeds, I see a tall blue bird looking up at the sun. I look over at Grandpa who is smiling and he says, "You found him." We sat watching the heron until its wings opened and he lifted up to the sky.

At that moment, we heard a beautiful sound. I say, "Grandpa! The loons are calling! We must go find them." We steer the canoe toward the loon call and I look through my binoculars, hoping to spot them first. I see a black spot on the lake getting larger as we paddle closer and realize the loon is straight ahead. My grandpa stops paddling and we coast through the water and stay as still as we can. We see one loon to the right of the canoe and one loon to the left of the canoe but there seems to be something else I see. As we get closer, my grandpa whispers to me, "There is a baby loon riding on its mother's back."

I look through my binoculars and see a small, brown, fuzzy, loon who is resting on the back of his mother.

Suddenly, one of the loons disappears into the water and I wonder where it went. As I squint to see across the lake, I see all three of the loons in Heron's Cove. They start talking as if they are sharing a story with Grandpa and me. "I wonder what they are saying," I say. My grandpa tells me loons use different types of calls depending on what they are trying to say. He says, "Let's just listen for a while," and as we sit in the canoe listening to the loons, I wish this day would never end.

Later in the day, I look down on the dock and see my
grandpa looking out at the smooth and sparkly water.
I start down the stairs to the dock and take a seat next to
my grandpa. He is smiling and I ask him why. He says,
"Do you like coming to Pine Lake?" I say, "I really like
it here, Grandpa, and I hope we can come here forever."
"Me too, my dear, me too," he says and he holds my hand
as the sun lit up the lake with bright, beautiful colors.

At bedtime, I ask Grandpa what he learned from Pine Lake today. He says, "I learned I will never stop being amazed by the beauty of this place." He asks me what Pine Lake taught me today. I say, "Pine Lake taught me this is a place where I belong, and it is a place I love." My grandpa smiles, turns off the light, and says good night. I close my eyes and hope my dreams are filled with tomorrow's adventures on Pine Lake.

Thank you to each person who provided guidance and support in their own unique way during this journey.